Bug Girl

Carol Sonenklar

Illustrated by Betsy Lewin

Henry Holt and Company
New York

Henry Holt and Company, Inc., *Publishers since 1866*
115 West 18th Street, New York, New York 10011

Henry Holt is a registered trademark of Henry Holt and Company, Inc.

Published in Canada by Fitzhenry and Whiteside Ltd.,
195 Allstate Parkway, Markham, Ontario L3R 4T8.

Library of Congress Cataloging-in-Publication Data
Sonenklar, Carol.
     Bug Girl / Carol Sonenklar; illustrated by Betsy Lewin.
         p.   cm.
     Sequel to: Bug Boy.
     Summary: When Charlie, having used his Amazing Bug-A-View to transform himself once more
into a bug, almost gets pinned to a bug board, his friend Suzanne turns herself into an ant and
comes to his rescue.
     [1. Insects—Fiction.   2. Magic—Fiction.]   I. Lewin, Betsy, ill.   II. Title.
     PZ7.S6977Bv   1998   [Fic]—dc21   98-3145

ISBN 0-8050-5821-4
First Edition—1998
Printed in the United States of America on acid-free paper. ∞
10   9   8   7   6   5   4   3   2   1

To my own little bug girl, Emma
—C.S.

For Juliana Simon-Fox
—B.L.

Contents

Going Buggier

There I was, crouched in a dark corner. I was invisible; perfectly camouflaged in the leaves and branches. My deadly assault was feared far and wide. Nothing could get by me.

And then I spotted something. Something desirable. Something delicious. It had no idea that just a few inches away, a hunter was lurking. My forceful arms and legs, alive with sensory vibrations, were itching to move. When I was ready to trap it in my death grip, I could bound at superspeed.

I was . . . a killer.

Meet Charlie Kaplan, assassin.

Assassin *bug*, that is.

The tantalizing termite poked its head out and I pounced. It was still struggling when I raised my sharp, tubelike proboscis and aimed for the meaty middle part, the thorax. Quickly, I sucked down the insides for a delicious morning snack.

Yum. Tastes like chicken.

Then I heard my mother call me.

"Charlie, where are you?"

I couldn't answer. Everyone knows that it's rude to speak with your proboscis full.

"You're supposed to be baby-sitting at the Dimarians'!"

Slurping up the last delicious bit, I scampered past the small termite mound, regretting that I couldn't hang around and munch on a couple more. I dashed back to the evergreen bush and made my way through the branches. My supersensitive antennae were moving and grooving constantly, so I could feel, hear, and see what was ahead of me.

As I scrambled through the branches, my antennae were picking up the scent of another tasty nearby snack—a crunchy little aphid—but I had to ignore it. My mom was getting annoyed that she couldn't find me these days, even though I was usually right under her nose (or foot, rather). I

detected a beam of light in front of me and headed for it. When I felt something cold and hard, I knew I'd found the Bug-A-View.

And then I was back. Sitting in the middle of the evergreen bush on top of the Bug-A-View. The Bug-A-View isn't something that bugs you when you view it (like, say, my little sister, Lucy); it is an incredible gift that I got from my best friend, Suzanne Dimarian. She saw it in a store somewhere and bought it for me as a joke. It looks like a flashlight with a magnifying glass. You look through it and press the little button on the outside, and it lights up what you're looking at. If you happen to be looking at a bug, it has a special feature . . .

It turns you into that bug.

This added feature, which Suzanne didn't know about, is only mentioned near the little button, where it says in teeny, tiny words: *See the World from a Bug's-Eye View!*

Pretty funny, huh?

So funny, I forgot to laugh.

The first time I looked through the Bug-A-View, I turned into my pet cobweb spider, Spidey. I didn't know what had happened until I lifted one of my hairy legs and realized I had seven more. Luckily I

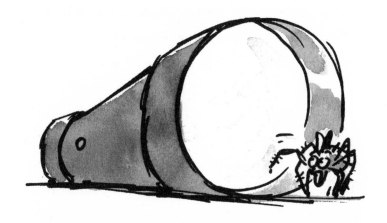

discovered that if I, as a bug, crawled back onto the lighted glass part at the end of the Bug-A-View, I'd transform back into a boy.

A boy who loves bugs.

And now that I have the Bug-A-View, I spend countless hours *being* a bug. Before, I was always on the outside, but now I get to be on the inside and—*whew!*—it can get pretty scary in there. It's a place where lightning-fast assassin bugs are feared killers, bombardier beetles drop acid bombs, and spiders paralyze their prey and eat it for supper.

All my life I wondered what it would feel like to have six or eight legs and superinsect powers. Now I know—I've been a little brown walking stick camouflaged on a branch, a green striped stinkbug stinking out a fly, and a colorful grasshopper soaring over the head of a deadly praying mantis. I've also been a deadly mantis, a stinging yellow jacket, and an angry biting red ant. To survive in this jungle, I have to follow some of my nastier insect instincts, which often means—eat or be eaten.

So you can see, it's not all fun and games. Aside from developing a taste for termites, I've had many close calls. Once I lost the Bug-A-View and had to plunge my little fly body into a disgusting garbage heap to find it. Another time I transformed into Spidey at school and just missed getting bombed by a bombardier beetle. The worst of all was when I had to run for my life to escape from my teacher's high heels. She wanted to turn me, Charlie Kaplan—one of her favorite students—into spider goo.

No one else knows about the magic powers of the Bug-A-View. But today that's going to change. When I'm finally alone with Suzanne, I'm going to tell her. Suzanne has always been my bug pal; she loves the little critters as much as I do. But now she has these two sissy girlfriends who can only say "Eeeww!" and run away when they see a creepy-crawler. Since she hangs around with them a lot, we haven't done much bug hunting lately.

That's why I'm going to tell her about the Bug-A-

View today. I just can't keep it a secret any longer. When she finds out about it, she might be scared at first, but then I know she'll want to try transforming too. Suzanne never wants to be the first to try anything; she'd rather wait to see what happens to someone else.

Boy, I can't wait to see her face when I transform in front of her.

She'll be bug-eyed.

A Bug in Suzanne's Ear

"**D**id you forget you told Suzanne that you'd help baby-sit Willie this morning before the field trip?" asked my mother, standing over by the evergreen bush.

I shook my head, keeping the Bug-A-View behind my back.

"Why are there branches in your hair?" questioned my six-year-old sister, Lucy, whose mission on earth is to get me in trouble.

"I'm going over to the Dimarians' right now, Mom," I said, casually running a hand through my hair. Some leaves fluttered down to my T-shirt. I quickly picked up my backpack and started across the lawn, avoiding my mom's eyes. "See you around dinnertime," I shouted.

Slipping the Bug-A-View under my shirt, I walked fast down the block. I was really excited today because our fourth-grade class was going on a field trip to "bug camp" at Heidi's house in the country. Heidi MacIntosh, an entomologist who works at the university, has major "bugs on the brain" like me. We're great friends, and she lets me help her in her lab sometimes. Maybe one of these days I'll bring the Bug-A-View to her lab and turn into a giant Australian walking stick or a hissing cockroach.

"Hey, Charlie! Come here for a second."

I turned to see Raymond Wintertree sitting on his front step, holding a magnifying glass. Next to him was a peanut butter jar.

Raymond was the class Goody Two-shoes. He always loved to report on what I was doing when it wasn't what I should be doing. And because he lived two houses down from us, his report would often make it to my parents. I wasn't really a troublemaker, but sometimes I'd find a little critter on the playground who was much more interesting

than, say, how many times 7 goes into 287. And sometimes that little buggy would find its way over to Raymond's leg in no time at all, and he'd jump up and yell "Eeeww!" just like the sissy girls.

And then I'd be sent off to "chat" with Mr. Baxter, the principal, who liked to tell me that if I didn't learn my math, I'd be an exterminator instead of an entomologist.

Ever since my bug adventure at school, though, Raymond's been better. That's because he's developed "bugs on the brain" too. But even on a warm Sunday afternoon like today, he was still dressed as if he might have to dash off to a piano recital. He was wearing a white dress shirt buttoned all the way up to his neck. I stuck the Bug-A-View in my pocket and jogged over to where he was sitting.

"Look!" He pointed to a beautiful green lacewing perched on the edge of a bush. These days, whenever I saw a new insect, it was hard for me not to pull out the Bug-A-View and . . . well, you-know-what.

"That's a beauty," I said.

"I'm going to get it for my collection," he remarked as he leaned over and tried to cup it in his hands. But it was too fast for him. He stomped his foot in frustration.

"I gotta go, Raymond," I said as I walked away. "See you on the field trip."

Even I was impressed with Raymond's growing bug collection; just last week he'd found a large stag beetle, and they're not that common around here.

I got to the end of the block, turned the corner, and took a shortcut to the Dimarians' house. I reached the edge of their yard and hopped over the bushes. Suzanne was sitting on the grass near a dirt patch while her little brother, Willie, was pushing some trucks around.

"Hi!" I yelled, plopping myself down on the ground next to her. "I've got something important to tell you."

Willie ran over to me. He was holding his favorite cup, which he carries with him everywhere. "Cha-wee! Cha-wee!" he shouted.

That's Willie's name for me. "Hi, Willie. What're you doing?"

"Doze-doze." He pointed to his bulldozer. Then he pressed a button on it, and it pushed some dirt. "Wew-wee push doze."

Willie is two. Suzanne's mother sometimes lets us baby-sit while she works in the house.

"That's great, Willie." I was impatient to talk to Suzanne. "Suzanne, listen. I've *really* got to talk to you."

Suddenly I felt the Bug-A-View leave my back pocket, and I quickly turned around.

Willie was holding it.

"Whazzis, Cha-wee? Whazzis?"

I grabbed it from Willie and said, "No!" He looked disappointed and turned back to his bulldozer.

"Why did you bring that thing?" Suzanne asked.

"This is what it's about. The something important."

She laughed, and her red curls bobbed around her head. "*That?* That's a joke, remember? I got it for you."

I shook my head. "It's not a joke. It's got . . . magic powers."

Puzzled, Suzanne looked at me. "Charlie, what's with you? It's a piece of junk. You said so yourself."

"I was wrong," I explained. "If you aim it at a bug and look through it, it transforms you . . . into the bug."

Suzanne narrowed her eyes. "Are you feeling okay? Did you have a weird dream or something? Did your mother make tofu pizza again last night?"

I shook my head. "It's true, Suzanne." I knew she wouldn't believe me, so I took a deep breath and did the only thing I could.

I aimed the Bug-A-View at the first bug I saw and pressed the button.

Down on the Ground! It's Superbug!

Suddenly I was in the trenches, surrounded by mountains of dry dirt. Wow. I scrambled up the side of a dirt mountain to get closer to Suzanne.

"Charlie? Where'd you go?"

Whoops, I forgot to tell her that while I'm a bug, I can't talk.

"Charlie?"

I was right in front of her face. Hey! I'm the one in the suit of armor. The pill bug!

"C'mon, Charlie. I'm not looking for you anymore."

Then I reared back, took a running start, and leaped onto what I think was her ankle. I was discovering that pill bugs don't see well at all; everything was grayish and blurry. My antennae helped guide me.

What's this little ball of dirt on me?" Suzanne shouted.

Hey! I resent that! A pill bug might look like dirt, but it's our best defense against predators and—jeez—we could use all the help we can get. We're not known for our speed or grace, but we've managed to stay alive for millions of years. So hey, let's show some respect!

But instead of respect I got brushed off into a pile of dirt. Now I was submerged in darkness. I had to get out. I tried to move, but it seemed very complicated. The dirt was heavy and moist—it was like trying to move your legs after you've buried them in the sand. And now I had twelve of them.

I dug and clawed through the dirt; it was endless. I had to stop and rest for a minute. I sensed something moving near me. It was a giant light-colored blob. And then the earth moved under me and I was scooped up into the air. Yah! What was happening?

"Doze get bug," Willie said.

I could be wrong but I think Willie is trying to pick me up. No way, Willie boy, not *this* pill bug. I dove down into the dirt, burying myself as much as I could. But Willie was digging through it. His gigantic pink fingers were like a human rake, surrounding me on both sides. I was about to be scooped up!

"Buggy," Willie whispered.

Oh, no, what could I do?

Then I suddenly remembered—the pill bug's superpower. I can become a living ball! I lay down on my side and curled everything in around my head. Bye-bye, Willie. I rolled off Willie's hand and fell

back into the dirt, landing without a scratch. My body was sturdy, like a hard shell. This was fun. I was a human snowball or, I mean, a bug snowball or, well, you know what I mean.

"Where buggy go?" Willie asked Suzanne.

"Where'd Charlie go?" Suzanne asked Willie.

Then Willie started to cry. "Wew-wee want buggy back."

"Aw, it's okay, Willie. I'll get you a buggy," Suzanne said.

Something enormous shook the ground. I heard

some grunts and groans and then the earth moved—
again! I was thrown out of my ditch to another part of
the dirt desert.

"Here, Willie. I rolled the stone over for you,"
Suzanne said. "There's lots of buggies there."

"Ooh, buggies," Willie chirped. "Whazzis?"

"Willie! You shouldn't touch that thing; it be-
longs to Charlie. Put it down," Suzanne said firmly.

I suddenly realized what was happening. Willie
had picked up the Bug-A-View and I couldn't do anything to stop him. It was quiet for a few seconds, but
then I heard something that made my little pill body
shiver—a loud gasp from Suzanne and then in a
small and shaking voice,

"Willie? Where are you?"

There was no answer.

Because, I knew, there was . . . no Willie.

A Little Slug Who Needs a Hug

"Help, Charlie!" Suzanne shouted. "Willie's gone! You're both gone!"

I sprang into action. But considering that I was a crusty little eighth-of-an-inch pill bug, that didn't amount to much. I had to transform back, but Willie had moved the Bug-A-View. I knew it couldn't be far away. Clambering to the top of a dirt hill, I looked around as best as I could.

Dirt, dirt, and more dirt.

I could hear Suzanne running around the yard in hysterics, looking for Willie. I tried to stay calm and think. Willie had to be nearby. Dashing past an ant, I quickly circled the surface of the rock. On my last lap around, I saw something yellow a little ways

24

over. Pulling in my legs to become a ball, I flung myself off the rock and tumbled until I hit a hard surface. Ouch!

My antenna senses told me it was the bulldozer. Talk about luck! The Bug-A-View should be close by.

As I swerved around the bulldozer, I stepped into a beam of light. I hoped it wasn't some kind of heavenly light, if you know what I mean.

But as I got closer, I saw that it was the Bug-A-View.

I crawled on top of the glass and . . .

Shazam!

"Suzanne! Wait!"

She had the back door open and was ready to step inside. I raced up to her.

"Charlie, where have you been?" She was breathing hard and trying not to cry. "This is so terrible. Something's happened to Willie. He's gone!"

"No, he's not gone," I replied between gasps. "I was trying to tell you—or rather, show you. The Bug-A-View is magic. It turns you into a bug."

She was staring at me, trying to understand. "What?"

"I haven't been gone. I've been here the whole

time, except that I was a bug. A pill bug. The one on your ankle."

She continued staring, scrunching up her face. "So . . . you were a bug? A pill bug?"

I nodded.

Then suddenly her face became terrified. "But what about Willie?"

I didn't answer. Instead I ran over to the dirt pile; Suzanne was on my heels. She made a lunge for the Bug-A-View, but I caught her arm.

"No, Suzanne. You have to leave it there. Otherwise he won't be able to find it."

"He?" Suzanne's eyes were wide. "Where is he? *What* is he?"

I didn't know what to say. I felt like a louse. Maybe I should become one as punishment.

"Charlie! Answer me! Where is Willie?"

Now *I* felt like crying. "I—I'm not sure."

She had her hand over her mouth. "Oh, my God."

There were tons of bugs crawling around. And more, probably, crawling away as we stood there. Willie could be any of them. Why did I show her the Bug-A-View with Willie around? While I was transformed into a bug, anything could happen with the Bug-A-View — I should've remembered that from before.

"How does th-that horrible thing work? How do you become human again?" Suzanne asked as she glanced in the direction of the Bug-A-View, almost afraid to even look at it.

"You have to get on the end of the glass. The lighted part," I explained.

"How's he going to know that?"

"He's not," I admitted, feeling even more louselike. "We have to find him and put him on the light."

"But how do we know which one is Willie?"

I couldn't answer that, so I knelt down very carefully in the dirt. How could I possibly know which bug he was? Should I go back to being a pill bug to try to find him? But pill bugs don't have the kind of antennae or senses that other bugs do. It would probably just complicate matters right now. Suzanne was near me, tentatively scooping up bugs and inspecting them. We went on like this for a while, neither of us talking.

And then another voice broke the silence. I heard five words that filled me with fear.

"It's time for Willie's nap!"

Suzanne and I looked at each other, horror-struck.

"Mom," Suzanne whispered in a garbled voice.

"I know," I garbled back.

"What are we gonna do?"

"Yoo-hoo! Kids!" Mrs. Dimarian stuck her head out the back door. "Where's Willie?"

"Uh . . . uh . . ." Suzanne's voice was several notches higher than normal. "He's over there, Mom. Near the dirt pile. You can't see him from the house."

I piped up to help out. "We're having such a great time out here, Mrs. Dimarian. Could Willie stay outside five more minutes?"

"Okay," she agreed. "But just five. When he's overtired, he gets a little antsy."

Suzanne and I gasped.

I lay down on the dirt pile, put my head next to a couple of little brown ants running around, and whispered, "Willie? Are you there?"

Suzanne was next to me, picking up handfuls of dirt. I motioned to a fat beige-reddish worm in front of her. "Go on. Talk to it."

"I have to talk to the worm?"

"It might be your brother," I reminded her.

"Willie! If you can hear me, nod your head up and down." Suzanne paused, then looked at me. "I think it's nodding. What do you think?" she said.

I didn't think so, but I didn't want to disappoint her.

"Oh, this is ridiculous, Charlie. How do you even know worms have ears?"

"I don't know," I replied. "But we have to take the chance."

She scowled at me and moved on to another worm.

Soon there was noise at the back door.

"Bring Willie in, please. It's nap time!" Mrs. Dimarian shouted.

Suzanne grabbed my arm hard. "Charlie! What are we going to do? There's bugs and worms all over the place — he could be anywhere!"

I didn't know what to do. Or say. Then I heard the back door slam. Mrs. Dimarian was on her way over. Suzanne's eyes were closed; her face looked white. My heart was pounding. I felt like we were in a scary movie, but the scary part hadn't come yet and we were just waiting, knowing it was going to come, which made it even more scary. I closed my eyes.

Mrs. Dimarian was coming closer. "Suzanne, where's Willie? Is he playing hide-and-seek?" Then there was a pause. "What is that . . . *thing?*"

I opened my eyes. Mrs. Dimarian was staring down at Willie's cup, looking horrified. "EEEWW! There's a brown slug on Willie's cup."

"It's him!" Suzanne blurted, then clamped her hand over her mouth.

Mrs. Dimarian didn't seem to hear. "I better get rid of this creature." She picked up the cup and started for the house.

"Wait!" Suzanne yelled. "Where are you going?"

"To the bathroom. I'm going to flush it down the toilet."

Suzanne and I looked at each other, panicked.

"Wait, Mrs. Dimarian!" I yelled. "I'll get rid of it. I love slugs, remember?"

"Yeah, they're so cute," piped up Suzanne, taking the cup from her mother and giving it to me.

"Cute?" echoed Mrs. Dimarian.

"And they're good for the environment," I added, making my way back to the dirt pile.

After I pulled the slug off the cup, I leaned down and whispered, "Don't worry, Willie. You'll be a kid again in a second."

I dashed over to the Bug-A-View, made sure my back was to Mrs. Dimarian, put Willie the slug on the lighted glass, and pressed the button.

When I turned around, Suzanne was pointing at the roof of the house in an attempt to distract her mother. Then Willie was back.

"Mama!" he sobbed loudly.

"Willie!" Mrs. Dimarian exclaimed. "There you are! Where were you hiding? Behind the oak tree?"

Willie ran to her and threw his arms around her legs.

"Me buggy, Mama. Wew-wee buggy," he cried.

"You're buggy?" said Mrs. Dimarian with a big smile, leading him into the house. "No, you're not. You're Willie. My favorite boy."

We could hear his little voice growing fainter as he went inside. "Me buggy, Mama."

I looked at Suzanne. She had her eyes closed and was taking deep breaths. I picked up the Bug-A-View and ran over to her. She raised her hands.

"No way, José. Get that thing away from me."

"So I guess you finally believe me now, huh?"

Backing off, she flicked her eyes at the Bug-A-View and then looked away. "Yes. Absolutely. That thing turned my little brother into a slug.

His own mother was about to flush him down the toilet."

"I know. That was pretty scary," I agreed. "But once you know how to use it, it's safe." I wasn't quite sure of this last statement, but I forged ahead.

"You gotta try it. It's incredible! You won't believe what it feels like to zoom through the air or weave a sticky web or pounce on a termite or—"

"Are you nuts? I wouldn't use that thing if you paid me a million dollars!" she shouted, and then quickly lowered her voice. "You should get rid of it, Charlie. It's dangerous."

"I'm not going to get rid of it," I replied. "Okay, maybe I shouldn't have had it around Willie. But how did I know he'd pick it up?"

"Why didn't you stop him?" Suzanne demanded.

"Uh, because . . ." That was a good question.

And then I realized why — because at the time, I was transformed too. I gasped out loud.

"What?" Suzanne got a scared look on her face. "What now?"

"I didn't stop Willie because I was a bug at the exact same time *he* was," I said excitedly. "That means two people can transform at the same time."

She was already shaking her head. "No, no, no, no, no."

"Suzanne," I pleaded. *"Please?* I promise nothing will go wrong."

I put on my most sincere, innocent face, the one I put on the day my mom discovered a cicada in the ice cube tray. (I was trying to keep it fresh for my collection.)

She glanced down at her watch. "Hey! We have to get to school for the bus to Heidi's." Then she looked me in the eye. "Charlie, forget it. I will never use that thing. Never, ever, ever."

I wagged my finger at her. "Never say never."

A Bug Hunting We Go!

"**H**i, everyone! Welcome to bug camp!"

I looked out the bus window. Heidi was standing on her front porch steps with a big smile on her face. I jumped out of my seat; I couldn't wait to get off. I'd been looking forward to this day for a long time. Six whole hours devoted to bug hunting.

Suzanne was ignoring me. She wouldn't sit next to me on the bus because she didn't want to be near the Bug-A-View. She said that she couldn't believe I was bringing it on the field trip, where there would be tons of bugs. That's exactly *why* I was bringing it, so I could transform if I saw something really cool.

Now she just gave me a snotty look as we headed

over to Heidi's porch. She was sticking to Shannon and Amber like glue. Raymond caught up with me. He was dressed more casually today in a perfectly ironed striped T-shirt.

"I'm determined to find something for my collection," he said. "A walking stick or a grasshopper would be great."

Danny Borofsky motioned for us to be quiet as he snuck up behind Shannon. Then he yelled, "Eek! A creepy-crawly caterpillar!" and dumped some grass down the back of her shirt. Shannon's scream probably woke up any nearby snoozing bats. Danny's humor wasn't appreciated by most of the girls in our class. I did, though, notice Suzanne covering her mouth; she didn't want Shannon to see that she thought it was funny.

"Okay, guys, have a seat on the lawn and listen up," announced Heidi.

She was wearing silver dragonfly earrings and a butterfly baseball cap. I sat down next to Raymond and Danny. Suzanne was standing off to the side; I could tell that she didn't know who to sit with — me or the sissy girls. Then Amber motioned for her to sit down, and she sat with them. That's okay. I didn't need her.

"Today we will be doing several different bug activities," Heidi said. "The first thing we must do is collect insects. I have some nets that I'll hand out. You can look anywhere for bugs — in the woods, near the pond, around the porch. We'll collect for a while and then later go into the cabin to pin and identify. Any questions?"

"You mean we get to stick pins in bugs?" Danny asked.

"Please raise your hand if you have a question or comment, Daniel," our teacher, Mrs. Solomon, remarked.

"I can't stick pins in bugs. I'll get sick," said Amber.

Heidi smiled. "You can just watch, okay?"

Everyone laughed, but Amber looked mad. Then Raymond leaned over to me. "I'm in luck. I brought my collection in my backpack because I wanted to show it to Heidi. Now I can just pin whatever I find right into it."

I nodded. "Good thinking, Raymond." What I had in *my* pack was about three million times better, but of course, I kept quiet.

"What if we don't find anything?" asked Shannon.

"Oh, you'll find something," Heidi answered. "But if anyone needs help, just ask me, Bug Boy, or Suzanne. I guess we should call you Bug Girl, right?"

Suzanne shrugged, looking down at the ground. She didn't look too sure about that. Shannon was wrinkling up her nose while Amber was pretending to stick her finger down her throat.

Heidi motioned to me to help her pass out nets. After we finished, we split off into smaller groups and started walking around. Suzanne, Shannon, and Amber were ahead of me and Raymond.

Danny was stuck walking with Mrs. Solomon, who had brought enough gear for a two-week trek into the Himalayas. She'd just finished spraying bug repellent over every square inch of her body, and now she hooked a canteen and compass to her belt.

I veered off into the woods to see what I could find. I didn't really want to be with anyone since I might use the Bug-A-View. Raymond headed toward the pond. I walked for a little while and then knelt down by some goldenrod. There was a striped tiger beetle peeking around one of the flowers. I quickly pulled out my jar and got ready to pick him up.

40

"Eeeww! That's soooo gross! I can't believe you're holding it, Suzanne."

Startled, I dropped my jar and looked up. Shannon and Amber were sitting on some big rocks having their snack; Suzanne was a little ways off, crouched over a log.

"It's just a little grasshopper," Suzanne replied.

"An ant just took a piece of my peanut butter cookie," exclaimed Amber.

Suzanne leaned forward, her hands still cupping the grasshopper. "Look how the ant is carrying the crumb over its head. That's so neat."

"No, it's not," said Shannon. "It's disgusting."

Amber bent over and dropped the rest of her cookie on the ground. "It's sort of disgusting but sort of neat too," Amber said.

Suzanne peered down. "Look! Another ant's taking a large piece of the cookie back to her colony. She'll be a hero to all the other ants for finding so much food."

"*She?*" echoed Shannon. "How do you know it's a she?"

"Because almost all ants are females," Suzanne answered. "The guys are around for just a few months to make more queens and then it's 'see ya around, buddy.'"

Amber and Shannon giggled.

"So it's only girls in the colony?" Amber asked.

Suzanne nodded. "Ant colonies are pretty cool. There are different rooms inside—one for the eggs, one for the larvae, and one for storing food. There's even a nursery."

"So there are baby-sitter ants?" Shannon asked.

I laughed out loud. All three girls turned and then scowled at me.

"Eavesdropping, Charlie?" Suzanne said with a huff and a frown.

I shook my head. "I wasn't, really. I was looking for a bug."

"Look." Suzanne pointed. "More ants."

"Let's make a trail," I suggested, heading over to the insects.

I pulled out a couple of graham crackers my mom had packed and gave one to Suzanne. She crumbled it up and spread around the crumbs.

"There they are." She pointed at the line of ants. "Word travels fast in the ant world."

"Especially about food," I added.

The four of us followed the ants for a while in and around the log. There were about twelve of them, all carrying bits of graham cracker high above their heads.

"It's hard to believe those little ants can carry such big crumbs," Suzanne remarked.

"I know," I agreed. "That's one of their superpow- ers — that they can carry ten times their weight. Their other superpower is teamwork. They commu- nicate with each other by passing special chemicals through their antennae. That's how they can kill larger insects and take them apart to carry back to the colony for food."

"Please." Shannon had her hand on her stomach. "I just ate."

As we watched and followed, the ants crawled briskly through the grass, down a dirt patch, and over a mass of sticks and stones. They were heading toward the back porch of Heidi's cabin.

But then something caught my eye on a nearby tree trunk. I leaned closer. It was a large, tan beetle making its way down the bark. I'd never seen anything like it before.

"Suzanne, look!" I pointed to the beetle.

Her eyes widened. "Wow! It's beautiful. What kind is it?"

"I'm not sure." I held a small branch in front of the beetle. As it crept onto it, I saw that the beetle was about an inch long.

"This is exciting!" piped Suzanne. "What if it's a new species? Or something really exotic? Maybe it's a goliath beetle?"

"No, those are only in the tropics," I replied. "It might be a potato beetle. I've never seen one, but I know they're big and they move slowly."

"Come on," Suzanne said. "Let's show it to Heidi. She'll know what it is."

"No, wait a minute, Suzanne."

I looked back at Shannon and Amber; they weren't paying the slightest bit of attention to us. Then I looked again at the beautiful beetle on the branch. I knew a lot about bugs, but there were plenty I had never seen before. I didn't think this was a rare species, but it wasn't your everyday garden variety. And who knew when I'd get the chance to see one again? I told Suzanne I had to transform into this mysterious creature before it got away.

Unfortunately Suzanne didn't see it from my point of view.

"Forget it, Charlie! No way!"

"Why not? It'll just be a minute, I promise. You can transform with me. Let's find a bug for you."

"I told you I wouldn't try that thing in a million years," Suzanne said angrily. "I can't believe you'd want to use it after what happened with Willie this morning."

Then we heard Heidi's whistle. "Okay, gang, it's time to get your insects and gather around. I'll be passing out some poison solution to pour into your containers. This will quickly and humanely kill your insects. Then we'll start pinning."

"Oh, shoot," Suzanne exclaimed. "I left my grasshopper in my jar over by the log. I'll be back in a second, Charlie.

"Charlie?"

I couldn't answer because I'd whipped out the Bug-A-View, aimed it at the beautiful beetle, and was now trying to balance myself on the tree branch. But it was trickyyyyy!

I grabbed on to the underside, but I missed and fell. Whatever kind of beetle this was, it was sort of a klutz. Now I was on the grass, about an inch from what I imagine were Suzanne's high-tops. I looked around for the Bug-A-View but didn't see it. With all the excitement, I guess I didn't plan this transformation too well.

Oh, brother.

"Charlie?"

I started to crawl on Suzanne's shoe to get her attention, but she must have taken a step.

Hey! Wait a second! Stop!

Now I was holding on to the side of her shoe with two legs. The rest of me was dangling off.

"Oh, Charlie! Not again!"

Her shoe stopped moving, and I got on top of it and jumped up and down.

"You dummy," she whispered. "You shouldn't have done this now."

Just then I heard a familiar voice.

"What are you doing, Suzanne?" Raymond asked. "Did you drop something?"

"Uh, I'm looking for a bug," Suzanne answered. "I haven't found one yet."

"I found a ladybug. But I'm not too excited about it since I already have one in my collection," Raymond replied. "Now I'm just trying to find the bathroom. Heidi said it was through the back door."

"Yeah, well, I'll see you inside, Raymond."

I could tell Suzanne was trying to get rid of him.

"Save me a place next to you for pinning."

"Okay. See ya."

Suddenly a spaceship-sized something came crashing down, missing me by inches. Then another! Leaping off Suzanne's shoe, I scampered up the nearest tree. I could now make out that the two spaceships were both dark and very shiny.

"Ouch, Raymond! You stepped on my toe!"

"Oh, sorry, Suzanne," Raymond said. "I thought I saw something on the ground."

I froze on the tree, knowing I'd attract more attention by moving. Come on, Raymond, go to the bathroom already. I need Suzanne to get me back to the Bug-A-View. I now realized that the tree I was on had a smooth surface. Out of nowhere, something pink appeared in the air next to me.

It was a face.

And that face was very much in *my* face even as I tried to get away from it.

Hey! Back off!

Then two pink moving sticks were heading straight for me. I knew they had to be fingers. I

darted up the tree, but they stayed with me. I swerved around to the other side to get away, but the fingers were closing me in. . . .

Caught! They lifted me up and brought me nose to nose, or rather nose to antennae, with my captor.

Yikes! It was Raymond! Up close and personal!

I struggled and squirmed and wriggled and writhed, but I couldn't get free.

"Hey, Suzanne! Look at this amazing beetle I just found on Heidi's porch rail!"

A Six-Legged Last Resort

Suzanne

I was repeating the words over in my brain: Stay calm, Suzanne. Don't panic. Don't stare at the beetle too much. Don't act as if you and the beetle have known each other since kindergarten or anything like that. Just walk over and take a quick peek.

"That's nice, Raymond." Good. Keep the voice steady. Composed. Nothing special.

"Is it rare?" Raymond asked excitedly. "I've never seen anything like it before."

He took a Jif extra-crunchy peanut butter jar out of his backpack and put — *gulp* — Charlie into it.

"No, no, no," I assured him. "That bug's not rare at all. They're all over these woods."

"So what is it, Suzanne?"

"What? Is it?" I took a deep breath. "Well, it's a . . . a . . . a *beige* beetle. A beige short-tailed beetle. A beige short-tailed herding beetle. Yep, that's what that little bugger is, all right, a beige short-tailed herding beetle."

"A herding beetle?"

Don't ask me what made me say that; my mouth had a mind of its own.

"Yeah. It herds other beetles together."

"And a tail?" Raymond echoed. "Beetles don't have tails."

"That one does. It's just really short. That's why it's called that."

Raymond looked skeptical. "Well, *I've* never heard of it. I'll have to ask Charlie. Where is he, anyway?"

I shrugged. "I think he went into the cabin."

"Then I'll ask Heidi."

"No, no, no, no, no," I gushed. "You don't have to ask Heidi. It's a short-tailed beige herding beetle. There's a picture of it in one of my bug books. And I know it said that these kinds of beetles are really common around here. *Really* common."

He gave me a funny look, which wasn't too

surprising, considering that I was babbling like an idiot.

"Well, I'm still going to show it to Heidi before I pin it."

"*WHAT?*"

I guess I reacted a little loudly. Raymond backed away about two feet.

"Are you okay, Suzanne?"

I nodded. "Yes, yes, yes. But *what* did you say? Something about pinning?"

He smiled. "Yeah. I'm going to use this beetle for pinning today. It'll be great in my collection."

My gaze dropped to Charlie in his hand. I swear he was on his knees, with his two front legs together. Praying.

"No, no, no, you can't do that."

"Why not?"

I had to think fast. There were too many things to think about at once. "Uh, because I have a grasshopper that would be perfect for your collection. Didn't you say that you'd always wanted a grasshopper?"

"No." He looked confused. "I don't think so."

"Sure you did—I remember," I insisted. "Well, you don't have one, do you?"

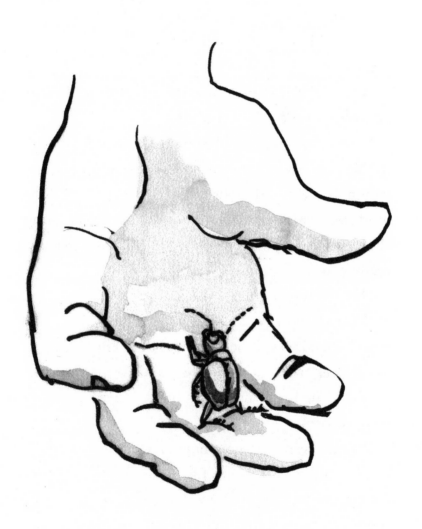

"No," he replied. "But I'd rather have this beetle."

"But how often can you find a grasshopper?" I persisted. "They're hard to catch."

"Yeah, I know," Raymond replied. "So why do you want to give it away?"

"Uh . . ." Think, Suzanne, think! "Because I know you really want it," I countered.

"But I *don't* want it," Raymond shot back.

"No, no, no, take it. And I'll just put this *very* common short-tailed herding beetle back in the wild with his thousands and thousands of other short-tailed beige herding beetle relatives that are really common around here."

"No," Raymond repeated. "I don't want it."

"Yeah, I know you don't want it. It's way too common." Boy, I was smooth. "Go ahead. The grasshopper is over there, near Shannon and Amber." I went to pluck the beetle out of his hand, but he suddenly stepped back.

"I don't want the grasshopper whether you want it or not, and I'm keeping the beetle for my collection, and right now I'm going to the bathroom," he said forcefully. Then he squinted at me. "Maybe you need to rest a little, Suzanne. You're acting weird."

He turned and went through the back door of the cabin. Suddenly I felt my heart start to beat fast. Charlie was trapped in a Jif jar. In less than an hour he'd be part of the bug collection. I had to save him.

Counting to twenty, I waited until I thought Raymond would be done in the bathroom. Then I ran inside. The class was going to do the pinning on the screened porch in the back. I stopped at the doorway. There he was, sitting on a high stool at the table, shaking the jar.

Oh, no. Was Charlie already gone?

I had to do something, but what? Then I had a brainstorm. I cupped my hands around my mouth and yelled, "What did you say, Heidi? You need someone to help you?"

Raymond's head snapped up. Whew, mission accomplished. I'd successfully activated his goody-goody reflexes. He put down the jar and jumped off the stool. I ducked behind the door as he ran past, then I sprinted over to the table and grabbed the jar.

But Charlie wasn't in there!

Frantically I looked on the table and then on the floor. He wasn't around. Raymond wouldn't have taken him with him, would he? I closed my eyes and thought: If I were Charlie, what would I do?

Then, suddenly, I knew. I unscrewed the cap of the jar and turned it over. There he was, grasping the airholes for dear life. One of his legs moved slightly.

"You big dummy. I've got you now," I whispered. "Don't worry."

"Suzanne!" Raymond shouted from the doorway. "What are you doing? Are you stealing my beetle?"

"N-no," I said feebly. "I, uh, just wanted to look at it. I wasn't sure if it was a short-haired jumping . . ." I couldn't even remember what I'd said before.

He scowled at me, yanked the cap out of my hand, and shook it hard, trying to get the beetle off the cap. But Charlie was hanging tough. "I don't know why I can't get him to fall."

Because in a minute there'll be a pool of poison under him, I wanted to scream. Instead I cleared my throat. "Want me to try?"

"No, thanks." He grabbed the jar and screwed the cap back on.

Then Heidi came in, followed by a bunch of kids. "We're going to have some quick lessons on how to pin. Please come up front and take a piece of foam board, an ID tag, and some pins."

Everyone moved to line up. I sidled over to Raymond, who was talking to Mrs. Solomon. The jar was on the table next to him. All I needed to do was nudge it an inch or two and cover it with my T-shirt.

WHOMP!

Raymond's hand came down hard on the jar. He yanked it away and cradled it against his chest.

"Bug off, Suzanne," he hissed as he walked away to get some foam board.

I stood there, frozen. I didn't know what to do. I couldn't get the jar away from Raymond, who was now keeping a very close watch on me. Maybe I should tell Heidi.

Then I remembered the Bug-A-View. It was out behind the cabin someplace. I had to get it before anything else happened.

"Suzanne," Mrs. Solomon called to me from across the room. "Where is Charlie?"

"Uh . . ."

"Tell him to get back here, now."

Good. An excuse to leave. "Sure. No problem." I was out the door in a nanosecond.

I remembered that Charlie and I had been talking near a big oak tree when he spotted the beetle. I crouched down outside the cabin, figuring the Bug-A-View had to be lying somewhere on the ground nearby. The ants were still there transporting stuff over their heads. Then a thought came to me — a scary thought that I immediately tried to put out of my head. But it was too late because it had already taken hold, and all the little switches and gears and motors in my head were turning it around.

And then my heart started pounding, and I got down on my hands and knees and followed the line of little brown ants. We went around a tree, past two big bushes, and then, as if it was all planned,

there was the Bug-A-View lying on the ground. I looked at it and silently told Charlie Kaplan that when I got his scrawny little body back, I would beat it up good for making the thought come back and flash in my brain like a neon sign.

And that thought was this: There was only one way to sneak into Raymond's bug collection and save Charlie. And that way was to just fit right in. By growing a leg or two.

Or four.

I took off my pink headband and tied it around a low branch so I could hopefully find this spot later. With a shaking hand, I picked up the Bug-A-View, keeping it at arm's length. I wasn't quite sure how this worked, and I didn't want to turn into brown mushroom fungus by mistake.

But what bug should I look at? A fly? A bee? Something with wings would be fastest, right? But I didn't see any of those around. I slowly lifted the Bug-A-View to my eye. Then I lowered it. I was too scared. The chances of staying alive for more than ten minutes around twenty-five fourth graders holding jars of poison solution were probably about a gazillion to one. I remembered that even with Charlie and me both searching, little Willie the slug was almost a goner.

But Charlie wasn't going to be able to hang on much longer. Time was running out.

And how could I, knowing about the Bug-A-View and its magic powers, do nothing to save him?

I had to do it.

I felt something ticklish on my leg and looked down. It was an ant. I took a deep breath and raised the Bug-A-View to my eye and pushed the button.

Charlie Kaplan, you owe me big time.

Or make that *bug* time.

Suz-ant?

H EEEEELLLLLLP!

Where was I?

Somebody, help!

Where's the Bug-A-View? I don't think it worked right. Something's wrong. All I can see is lots of little pictures of green stuff. It's like being inside a kaleidoscope. I have to get out of here. Fast!

I started to run, but my legs were like a bumper car that swerved and swayed and slipped and slid all over the place. I was losing my balance. I was going to crash into the green stuff!

Ouch! Now my bumper car legs are moving sideways, backward, diagonally, and every other way

64

through the prickly green stuff all around me. I'm trapped! I need air! I'm choking!

One, two, three. Stop. Get ahold of yourself, Suzanne. I squealed on the bumper car brakes.

Okay. Inhale. Exhale. I am breathing now. I am not hysterical now. I am calm now. I am cool now. I will lean over and investigate my legs now....

I'm going to pass out now.

The Bug-A-View really did work. I am an ant. I CAN'T DO THIS. I JUST CAN'T GO THROUGH WITH IT.

Inhale. Exhale. Yes, I can do this. I must do this.

I inched out my leg. Then another. Then another. Then another. Then another. Then the last one. I kept telling myself that if I moved slowly and carefully, I'd be okay.

I realized that the reason I was seeing lots of pictures of the same thing instead of just one picture of one thing was because ants, like most insects, have compound eyes, which are made up of lots of lenses. I could see up and down and all around at the same time but only in small pictures. Now that I was getting used to it, I could tell what the green stuff was: tall, thin blades of grass. I was in a grass jungle. Carefully I managed to wiggle through some stalks without toppling over. But now what? Where do I go?

Suddenly I knew. Don't ask me how or why, but I knew I had to crawl in a certain direction. I *must* go. I *must* obey. Obey? Obey who? What was this? Ant mind control?

I felt this command through my antennae, which were signaling all sorts of stuff: what lay ahead, whether there were any insects around, whether there was danger nearby. It was like having your eyes, ears, nose, and fingers all combined in one spot. And right now my antennae were telling me to move it.

One, two, one, two . . . what am I doing? I'm marching. Just like in "The Ants Go Marching" song. This is ridiculous!

I sure hoped that I was marching toward Heidi's cabin because I couldn't go in another direction even if I wanted to. It was as if I was programmed.

I'd made it through the grass jungle, and now I was on some dirt. It seemed as though I'd traveled a million miles. Tilting my head this way and that, I made out something enormous and white in front of me. I hoped it was Heidi's cabin.

I sensed activity and looked around. Yikes! Ants were coming at me from every direction. There were hundreds of them.

Then a large ant approached me. We touched our antennae together, and I could smell something. It smelled familiar somehow and (okay, this is going to sound weird) friendly. Don't ask me how a smell can be friendly, but it was. Suddenly I knew that it was okay, that this ant and I were friends.

Now we all marched together. One, two, three, four.

The steps. The steps of the cabin. We must go to the steps.

It's all making sense. The ant colony must be

under the steps. The queen is in the colony, which is why we're all being drawn toward it.

But I can't go. I have to stop. If I don't, I'll never get to Charlie. I had to resist the powerful ant mind control.

Focusing all my willpower, I slowly stopped. Whew. I fought my way through the crowd and managed to get to the edge of the cabin. My antennae were telling me, "Stop! Get back home where you belong!" But I had to ignore the thought. I crawled around the side of the cabin, searching for a crack.

I spotted a big one and started up the side.

Whoa. This made me feel sick. I saw the world completely sideways, yet I was as steady as on the ground. I scrambled up the side quickly and ducked into the crack. It was very dark, but luckily my antennae were guiding me, telling me it was safe to move forward.

Then a new message flashed: Alert! Alert! Danger nearby!

Oh, no. What was it? Should I turn around and leave? It was too late. A king-sized black carpenter ant lunged out of the darkness and grabbed my leg.

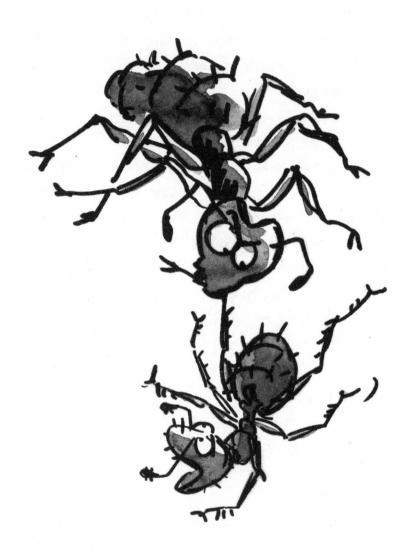

Ouch! Help!

I swooped down and bit at her antennae with my mandibles. But she was big and powerful and didn't let go. I could feel her sharp teeth around my leg, and I knew in a second she was going to bite it off. She was probably on a food mission for her colony in the walls of the cabin. I jerked my leg back and forth, trying to get it out of her grip. This was unbelievable: I was going to become lunch for a gang of bully carpenter ants.

But suddenly a cluster of brown ants jumped out from behind me and attacked her.

I could tell from their smell that they were from my colony. My ant buddies were coming to my rescue! They rushed onto the carpenter ant, some grabbing at her antennae, others pulling on her legs. In a few seconds she was retreating.

I approached one of the brown ants to do the antennae-speak: Thanks, guys! I think I got the message through. Then I started on my way, hoping I wouldn't run into any more carpenter ants.

After a little while, though, I sensed that again

I was not alone. I turned around, and about six of the brown ants were in a row behind me. I stopped moving. They stopped. I started again. They started again. I stopped again. They stopped again.

What were they doing?

I tried some antennae-speak. They were following me? They had to? They were obeying me? I was their . . . leader?

No, I tried to tell them. You're confused. I'm not a queen going to lay eggs. I'm just trying to . . . oh, well, it's too complicated to explain. If you guys want to come with me, I guess it's okay.

The troops and I crawled for a while. We were now deep inside what seemed to be a tunnel in the wall. My eyes must've been getting used to the dark because I made out wavy wood grain on both sides of me. I could hear voices—and then I remembered Charlie.

"Heidi, I can't find my bug."

"Heidi, one of my daddy longlegs' legs fell off."

"Heidi, the smell of the poison is making me nauseous."

"Be patient, everyone," Heidi replied. "I'll help you all."

"Class, does anyone know where Charlie and Suzanne are?"

Whoops. I guess I forgot that small detail.

"I saw Suzanne a few minutes ago, Mrs. Solomon," Raymond answered. "Heidi, can we start pinning?"

Whew! They hadn't started pinning yet; we still had some time. So even though it seemed like ten years since I'd become an ant, it had only been about ten minutes. You can make great time on six legs.

'Ten hut, troops!

We will proceed north.

Hup hup hup hup!

Marching on, we reached the end of the tunnel, and I stuck my antenna out for a look-see. We were up on a light-colored wall. It seemed safe. I inched out of the crack and started down. The troops followed. I crawled onto something silver that was in the middle of a big white thing. When I reached the end, I realized we must be on a water faucet in the sink.

I was trying to decide if we should head over

in the direction of the door when it slammed shut. Someone was in here with us.

I froze on the tip of the faucet. The troops froze too. I heard the sound of running water and then a loud whooshing noise. I didn't have to guess what that was—the toilet flushing. A sound that all insects feared!

The person moved over to the sink. I tried to direct the troops to turn back, but we weren't fast enough. Suddenly it was Niagara Falls.

Hang on, troops!

"Oh, darn, the drain doesn't work," Shannon muttered. "Eeeww, ants. Get off the faucet."

Now my antennae were going crazy, and the

hairs on my legs were doing the macarena. I was swept off into the air. Help!

I landed in an ocean in the sink.

I heard Shannon leave the bathroom as I kicked my little legs around, trying to tread water. But it wasn't working; I could feel myself getting limp, just wanting to relax and sink.

But then something grabbed my front two legs and pulled them forward. Something else pulled my two back legs backward. My body was being stretched out on the water's surface. I wasn't going under anymore. What was happening? Then I got a message through the antennae-speak: My troops had formed a chain with their bodies, and we were floating across the water to the side of the sink.

They saved my life! What a great bunch of gals.

When we finally made it to the other side of the sink, I spotted a crack that led from the sink to the wall.

No time to rest, girls.

I raced to the corner and darted inside. The porch was on the other side of the wall. Now I had to scout out the area for my troops. Any evil carpenter ants around? Diabolical termites? No, my antennae told me we were safe. I moved through the darkness. Voices were getting louder and louder. I stuck my antennae out into the light. Yep, this was the place.

The bug torture chamber.

The Porch of Destruction

I started down the wall, hoping we wouldn't be noticed. We reached the floor in three seconds flat. There were several long tables with stools; Raymond was sitting directly in front of us.

"Okay. Do you all have an insect in your jars?" Heidi asked.

"Yes!" shouted the class in unison.

"Good. We're finally ready to distribute the solution. Raymond will be coming around and pouring some into each jar," Heidi said. "This is acetone, otherwise known as fingernail polish remover. Remember that it is poison, so be careful."

Fall into formation, troops. We'll be climbing up the table leg.

I knew the coast would be clear where Raymond sat for a few minutes, so we zipped up the table leg and crawled onto the surface. In front of me was a big white board—Raymond's bug collection, otherwise known as the bug graveyard. But where was the jar? I tried to pick up signals from Charlie, but my antennae were overloaded from all the other warnings in the room: DANGER! ALERT! WATCH OUT! BEWARE! GET THE HECK OUT OF HERE, RIGHT NOW! As if I liked being here or something.

Then I spotted the jar on the other side of Raymond's bug collection. I darted over, my loyal troops right behind me. I was scared; this was enemy territory in a big way. I reached the jar and put my trembling antennae on it. Charlie, are you in there? Give me a sign.

But there was no sign. There was nothing.

"Pee-yew. This killing solution stinks," Danny hollered.

"Has anyone seen Charlie or Suzanne?" repeated Mrs. Solomon.

I started up the side of the jar. I had to get inside or at least to an airhole. But just then, everything got dark. A giant shadow was looming over me. I saw lots of little Raymonds, holding lots of little white cups.

Troops, retreat!

We darted back and positioned ourselves under a corner of the collection board. There was something crinkly hanging down from the edges. It must be plastic wrap. Plastic wrap had to be kept on collection boards so people wouldn't touch the bugs.

Raymond picked up the jar, opened it, and tried to shake Charlie down from the lid again.

"This short-tailed dummy won't come down," he muttered. "Well, he'll fall in a minute."

He poured some of the stinky stuff inside. I inched closer, sensing some motion in the jar, and waved my antennae wildly. Charlie, over here! It's me, Suzanne. The one with the head, thorax, and abdomen!

But I couldn't tell if he heard me because Raymond's giant pink hand came back down and covered the jar. No—don't put the lid back on! He moved the lid over the jar, lowered it, and had begun to screw it back on when suddenly Charlie jumped off. He was making a run for it!

"Hey!" Raymond exclaimed.

"What's the matter, Raymond?" Heidi asked.

"My bug just got away." Raymond sounded puzzled.

Charlie was on the tabletop, running toward us. Come on, Charlie, come on! Troops, prepare to shield and protect.

Then Charlie suddenly stopped, looked around, and turned left. I tried to scream through my antennae. That's the wrong way! After a few steps he stopped again, looked around, and started back toward the jar.

I knew what was happening. The fumes were confusing him, making him woozy.

Troops, full speed ahead. We must help Charlie.

I darted out from under the collection board. Charlie was weaving from side to side, moving in slow motion. Hold on, Charlie, we're coming! We were just about there when the hand of doom swooped down and picked him up.

"There you are," Raymond said. "What do you think you're doing? Trying to escape?"

Raymond was holding Charlie in one hand; in the other he held the open jar with the poison inside. Then he dropped him in. AAH!

But wait. It looked like Charlie got a foothold on the ridge at the top of the lid. He was hanging by a leg.

"Okay, gang," Heidi announced. "We're ready for pinning. Place your insect on the foam board."

Realizing that Raymond would be needing his collection board, I quickly led the troops to the edge of the tabletop. Peeking over, I watched Raymond open the jar again and pick Charlie off the top. I couldn't tell if Charlie was okay or not, but I knew he was good at holding his breath.

Raymond peeled back the plastic wrap and hunched over his board. He didn't bother with the solution anymore; he just put Charlie right down on the board to pin. I couldn't believe what was about to happen. I had to act fast.

There was only one thing left to do: Fall in line, troops. Forward, march!

We charged over to the edge of the board, and I leaped onto it. Raymond's enormous head was hanging over me.

Troops, stay out of the enemy's field of vision. Keep to the sidelines.

Charlie was straight ahead, just past the gar-

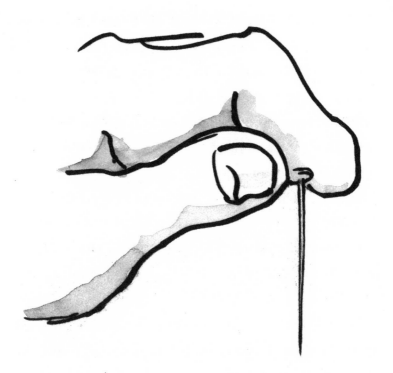

gantuan pink Mount Everest that must have been Raymond's nose. I crawled closer. Poised above my head were Raymond's thumb and forefinger, the deadly dagger between them. Then the fingers moved down, aiming straight for Charlie's abdomen. I was about to watch my best friend become shish kebab!

Troops, when I give the signal, create a diversion.

The pin was an inch from Charlie's shell. A half inch. A quarter inch.

One, two, three, NOW!

The troops took off, dashing around wildly all over the board. Raymond was so surprised, he dropped the pin.

"Hey! What's going on?"

Great work, girls. Keep moving. Keep the enemy distracted.

I ran over to Charlie. He wasn't moving. He was probably unconscious from the fumes. Now what? He was too big for me to move by myself, especially under Raymond's forty-foot nose.

"Get out of here, you dumb ants!" Raymond cried.

Fan out and take cover, troops. A weapon has been sighted.

Just then Raymond's pin fell down and hit a mummified grasshopper, splitting his exoskeleton in two. YIKES! I lurched under a nearby stag beetle corpse. The troops had scattered and were huddling under other specimens.

"No, I can't do it. I can't push that pin into the poor little mosquito," Mrs. Solomon was saying. "It's just too cruel."

"My gum fell into my killing solution," Shannon whined.

"My daddy longlegs is stuck to the pin," Danny mumbled.

I was planning our next tactic when suddenly there was a strange, crackling sound. I peeked out. Raymond was gone, but the sky had turned a sickly shade of yellow. Uh-oh, it was the suffocating plastic wrap. We were all trapped in here together now.

"Heidi." Raymond's voice was farther away. "I need help. There's all these little ants on my board, and I can't get rid of them."

"Just hold on, Raymond," Heidi said. "Wait one minute."

The Troops Pull Through

I knew that Raymond would be back with Heidi very soon, so this was it. Do or die. If we fail, we become ant guts and Charlie gets displayed on Raymond's bedroom wall next to piano recital awards till the end of time. I was scared. Really scared.

But then I saw Charlie lying there, looking just like the rest of the insect corpses, and I summoned my strength. I had to do it, not only for Charlie but for the girls, my trusty troops. I'd gotten them into this mess; I had to get them out. Glancing up at the yellow sky, I tried to stay calm. We can do it. We can rescue Charlie and get out of here alive. I just wasn't sure how.

I slipped out from under the stag beetle and crawled over to Charlie. He was completely still except for one little twitching leg. Ducking under his body, I took a deep breath. Now I would learn firsthand if ants could really lift ten times their weight.

I bent down and got a good grip with my antennae. Then I straightened up, lifting him off the ground, then higher and higher until he was above my head. Whoa! It's mega-ant. Weight lifter of the insect world!

Troops, start your retreat.

But my troops couldn't retreat. I'd forgotten about the plastic wrap coffin. Even if we wedged out between the board and the plastic wrap, there

was no way to carry Charlie out—he was too big. Desperately I pushed Charlie against the plastic wrap, trying to poke a hole with his pointy little head. It didn't work.

Oh, great. *Now* what?

"Thanks for being patient, Raymond. No, Mrs. Solomon, you're supposed to put the pin through the insect's abdomen, not its neck."

"Oh, my goodness. I've decapitated him!" shrieked Mrs. Solomon.

How could we get out of here? There had to be a way through the plastic wall. I looked around and spotted the pin that Raymond dropped when the troops fanned out. That just might make a hole for us to climb through.

I left Charlie on the board, crawled over, and picked up the pin. But I couldn't hold it; it was too skinny and kept falling through my antennae. I started crawling around in circles—thinking, thinking.

Something sharp jabbed my abdomen. I'd bumped into one of the clawlike pincers on the big stag beetle. Pincers! That's just what we needed. Ants chew apart larger insects to carry back to their colonies all the time. The troops could chew off the pincers.

I know this is gross, troops, but . . . ready, set, gnaw!

In no time at all the troops had gotten one of the stag beetle's pincers off. Then I hoisted it over my head, and went back to the edge of the board where we'd left Charlie. Okay, here goes nothing. I took a deep breath and plunged the pincer as hard as I could through the plastic wrap.

RRRRIIIP!

There was a slash of brilliant light. Hurray, troops, we did it!

"Who's next? Raymond?" asked Heidi.

Oh, no! They're coming!

I quickly lifted Charlie up and dashed over to the tear. Then I climbed on top of a skeletal stinkbug and heaved Charlie through the plastic wrap. Yes! He was out.

Now I was scrambling up and out of the plastic wrap myself. One of my feet slipped, but a trooper caught me and gave me a boost.

On top of the plastic wrap now, I picked up

Charlie and ran as fast as I could. When I reached the end of the board, I shoved him off and jumped.

My troops came barreling fast as we all ran for the table edge.

"Here's my board, Heidi," Raymond said. "What the . . . ?"

"Oh, my gosh. Is that a pincer sticking up through the plastic wrap?" Heidi asked.

"M-my stag beetle. It's broken." Raymond sounded like he might cry.

"I'm sure it just broke off, but it looks like"—
Heidi giggled a little—"a great bug escape."

"Where'd my beige short-tailed herding beetle
go?"

"Your *what?*"

Yes, sirree, I thought, as we made our way
down the table leg, carrying Charlie. So much for
those dumb little ants, huh, Raymond?

We hit the floor, running. We're going a different route now, troops. Follow me. With Charlie in
his present condition, I had to get back to the
Bug-A-View as quickly as possible. The fastest
way was directly across the floor, out the back
door, and down the porch steps. It was risky, but
we had no choice.

Hoisting Charlie high, we started across the
floor, dodging sneakers and swerving around
sandals. We leaped over a wad of bubble gum,
sidestepped Mrs. Solomon's calamine lotion, and
kept going. Come on, troops, we're almost there. I
could feel Charlie starting to move his legs. That
was a good sign; the farther we were from the
fumes, the faster he'd wake up.

When we had reached the doorway and zipped
down the porch stairs, my troops suddenly

stopped. I did the antennae-speak: What's up, girls?

Dinner was what was up. Specifically the dinner we were carrying—Charlie Kaplan, special of the day.

I should've known. My troops were just doing what they were supposed to do: get food for their hungry hordes at home. Now what?

But then I smelled something nearby, something sweet and edible—and it wasn't Charlie. Leaning over in the direction of the smell, I detected a nice big chunk of Amber's peanut butter cookie.

Chow has been spotted. Over here!

I motioned, and the troops dropped Charlie like a hot potato and headed for the cookie. Quickly I

hoisted Charlie back up and ran in the direction
of the Bug-A-View.

And then I spotted it. On the magnifying part
there was a beam of light, so the button on the
Bug-A-View was still pressed in. Phew.

I dropped Charlie onto the Bug-A-View and then
jumped on next to him.

This blasted thing better work....

"**W**hat ha — ?"

Charlie looked a little green, but that was about the worst of it. He was lying on the ground and I was sitting next to him, breathing a big sigh of relief. The Bug-A-View worked. I was Suzanne again.

"Suzanne!"

I turned toward him. "Yeah?"

"What happened? Did I pass out or something? The last thing I remember is looking at a strange bug—some kind of beige beetle." Charlie sat up and rubbed his head.

"The last thing you should remember is *becoming* that beige beetle," I retorted. "And I just saved your life. If it wasn't for me, you'd be the newest addition

95

to Raymond's bug collection. He'd hang you in the place of honor next to his Cub Scout macaroni Pledge of Allegiance."

"What?" Charlie looked at me openmouthed.

"You transformed into that beetle and then Raymond collected you. Don't you remember? He put you in a jar with some killing solution," I explained. "I had to rescue you."

"How?"

"I transformed," I answered. Charlie's mouth dropped open even wider.

"You transformed? Into a bug?"

"No, into a ham sandwich, brainiac. Yes, of course, into a bug. Into an ant, actually," I replied casually, as I grabbed my headband from the branch.

"An ant?"

"I tried to get you away from Raymond, but I couldn't," I continued. "I realized the only way to do it was to become a bug so I wouldn't arouse suspicion."

"I can't believe it," Charlie said weakly.

"Neither can I," I agreed. "But I did. My loyal ant troops and I crawled into Raymond's bug collection and got you out of there. It was a daring rescue mission," I added, in case he didn't figure it out himself.

He was shaking his head slowly. "I just can't believe it. You transformed. For me."

I eyed him warily. "Now don't get gushy on me, Kaplan. You owe me."

He narrowed his eyes. "What did you think of transforming?"

"Well." I took a deep breath. "Let's just say I'm not in a hurry to have antennae again anytime soon."

A voice in the distance suddenly called out, "Suzanne! Charlie! Where are you?"

"It's Mrs. Solomon." I stood up and offered Charlie a hand. "We'd better go."

With my other hand I reached down to grab the Bug-A-View. Charlie jumped backward like he'd seen a ghost.

"What's the matter?"

"Get that away from me," he exclaimed, looking in terror at the Bug-A-View. "It — it almost killed me."

"Well, I'm glad you've finally come to your senses about this thing, Charlie," I remarked.

"Let's get rid of it somehow. Leave it here or throw it in the pond or —"

"Bury it!" I piped up.

"Good idea," Charlie replied.

But neither of us moved.

"*You* bury it," he finally said. "I don't want to touch it."

"Okay," I agreed.

I knelt down and began to dig with my hands. Soon there was a little hole. I placed the Bug-A-View inside it, then covered it back up with dirt. Then I noticed some movement on the ground. I leaned lower to look. There was a small line of little brown ants crawling near my knee. They looked familiar.

"The troops!" I yelled, and turned toward Charlie. But he'd already started off.

"Hi, girls," I whispered to them.

I watched the ants march in their perfect little line toward the colony. It was absolutely incredible that not very long ago I was the leader of that line. Smaller than a pin.

Suddenly I ripped part of my headband. I turned back to where I'd buried the Bug-A-View and tied the piece tightly around some vines in the ground.

"Come *on,* Suzanne," Charlie yelled. "Let's get out of here."

I gazed down one last time. And then three little words flashed through my mind, and I knew that my troops were giving me one last antennae-speak:

Never say never.

Carol Sonenklar

Last year my daughter, Emma, and I attended a "bug zoo" day at Penn State University. We saw several beautiful Malaysian walking sticks. These light brown insects measure approximately three and a half inches long. When I noticed someone taking pictures of them, I suddenly got an idea to pose with one of the walking sticks and send it to my editor, Christy Ottaviano. Several days after I sent the photo, I was disappointed that I hadn't heard from her. I assumed she'd flip when she saw me with a giant insect in my hair. So I called Christy and asked her if she'd received the photo.

"Yes," she replied. "That was funny. Where did you get the fake bug barrette?"

Needless to say, she was a bit more surprised when I told her the truth!

Betsy Lewin

I've been stung by bees and wasps and bitten by spiders — all painful experiences. But I'll never forget
one night in a tent in Australia. I slid into my sleep-
ing bag, then shot out like a human cannonball,
roaring in pain. My big toe was on fire, and I
thought I'd been stung by a scorpion. I unzipped
the bag and spread it open. There sat a big, black
ant. I didn't chase it out of the tent. It chased me.